Enjoy my book katy!
From Granny Jean

Jack's
Midnight
Adventures

Jack's Midnight Adventures

Granny Jean

Illustrated by Ian R. Ward

Matador
9 Priory Business Park,
Wistow Road, Kibworth Beauchamp,
Leicestershire. LE8 0RX
Tel: 0116 279 2299
Email: books@troubador.co.uk
Web: www.troubador.co.uk/matador
Twitter: @matadorbooks

ISBN 978 1800461 468

British Library Cataloguing in Publication Data.
A catalogue record for this book is available from the British Library.

Printed and bound by CPI Group (UK) Ltd, Croydon, CR0 4YY
Typeset in 12pt Bembo by Troubador Publishing Ltd, Leicester, UK

Matador is an imprint of Troubador Publishing Ltd

Once upon a time (all good stories begin with once upon a time) there was a little boy called Jack who lived with his mummy and daddy in a cosy house. Jack loved his house because there was always a smell of lovely food coming from the kitchen.

One night it was very cold outside because it had been snowing; Jack was tucked up in his warm bed and smiled as he snuggled under his cosy duvet. Through the window he could see the snow on the rooftops and all the hundreds of stars twinkling in the sky.

Jack smiled; he was sure the stars were twinkling just for him and they were wishing him goodnight. He could see the big yellow moon and Jack was sure that the moon was smiling at him. Jack smiled back at the moon and fell asleep.

5

That night Jack had a wonderful dream. He dreamed that he could drive a big, big, big truck. Jack's truck was bright orange so everyone could see him coming. His truck was called Billy. Jack loved driving Billy up and down the motorways and through all the towns and villages. Everybody watched out for Jack in his truck, and they stood at the side of the road waving and clapping.

Jack's truck was full of lovely food which he took to all the shops. He took crusty bread, creamy milk, fresh eggs, meat, yummy puddings and everything else you can think of. All the people were pleased to see Jack and wanted to know what tasty food he had in his truck. Soon Jack's truck got too old to drive, so Jack put Billy in his garden so all the children could play on him and pretend they were drivers.

Then Jack dreamed he could drive a bus. It was the best bus in the world and Jack loved his bus. It was red, yellow, blue, green and purple with silver and gold stars that twinkled in the sunshine.

Jack called his bus Sally. Jack took people on rides in his bus and they came knocking on Jack's door asking where he was going to take them. He liked to take them to the seaside, and all the children, mums and dads used to play on the sand. They made sandcastles and splashed in the sea; they squealed because the water was cold.

Sometimes they went for a ride in the countryside. Jack showed them the lovely flowers in the fields and sometimes they saw the baby lambs with their mothers. All the people on the bus were singing and laughing. They asked Jack where they were going to stop for a picnic. Jack always took them to a big field. They ate delicious ham and cheese sandwiches, crisps, and sticky iced buns. Then the children played games and had races while the mums and dads sat on the grass and had a chat. Soon Sally was too old to drive, so Jack put her in his garden where the children could play.

Then Jack dreamed he could drive a big, big train. It was painted red and had shiny silver wheels. Jack loved his train and called him Freddie. Jack and Freddie went all over the country taking people on holidays to lovely places. Everybody loved Jack's train because it went very fast and made a whistling noise. It was special because it had beds for when people were going a long way and were feeling tired. One day the people asked Jack if he could take them to London. Jack was excited because he wanted to take the people to see all the wonderful sights. They had to get up early because London is far away. They had a wonderful time and were tired when they got back on Jack's train at the end of the day.

Jack had shown them Buckingham Palace where the Queen lives. He was SURE the Queen was looking through her curtains and was waving at them.

Soon Freddie was too old to drive, so Jack took him to a museum where they look after old trains and keep them shiny. Freddie was happy, because when the children came to the museum they could sit on the train and pretend they were going on holiday.

Then Jack dreamed he was a pilot. His plane was the best super jet in the world and it was called Johnnie. The people loved flying in Jack's plane because it was so smooth it hardly felt as if it was moving. Jack took people all over the world in his super jet. He took them to the other side of the world to Australia. There they saw kangaroos carrying their babies in pockets. Then they went to China where they had some delicious food. They didn't use knives and forks to eat their food; they used strange things called chopsticks. They weren't very good at that and the food kept dropping on the floor, so they had to use their fingers. Oh no!

Next they went to some countries where it was very hot. They went to Africa and saw lions and elephants. The lions looked fierce, but the elephants looked to be having a good time. Jack liked flying over the North Pole where he could see the snow and ice. Sometimes he could see Santa Claus feeding his reindeer and Jack would give him a wave. Soon Jack's super jet was too old to fly, so Jack put Johnnie in a big garage for old jets. Johnnie was happy when all the people came to look at him.

Then Jack dreamed he was an astronaut. He had the finest rocket that reached right up to the sky. All Jack's friends wanted to know where he was going in his rocket. Can you guess what Jack said?

"I AM GOING TO THE MOON, OF COURSE!"

His friends were very excited and told Jack to take care. They watched as Jack's rocket set off in a big, big puff of white smoke.

Jack loved it in his rocket. He could see the twinkling stars and he flew right over the moon. Wow!

When Jack woke up next morning after his wonderful dream he was still smiling. His mummy and daddy asked him why he looked so happy. Jack said,

"I HAVE FLOWN TO THE MOON AND ALL THE WAY BACK!"

Jean Mason was born in the small Yorkshire village of Darton. Educated at Wakefield Girls' High School and Hull Teacher Training College she has dedicated her life to the education of young children. After retiring from the teaching profession, she resolved to write a book based on the interests and imaginations of young children. Jack's Midnight Adventures, with its unique conception of a dream, is the first of a series.